HUMANO MORPHS

CAUTION: CONTENTS OF THIS BOOK MAY BE HAZARDOUS TO THE WORLD

T5-CUU-350

M. D. Spenser

Paradise Press, Inc.

Weston, FL

32124-3

To the real Amanda, Kelly and Maria,
for allowing their names to be used
in such an unpleasant manner.

Published by Paradise Press, Inc. by arrangement with River Publishing, Inc. All
right, title and interest to the "HUMANOMORPHS" logo and design are owned by
River Publishing, Inc. No portion of the "HUMANOMORPHS" logo and design
may be reproduced in part or whole without prior written permission from River
Publishing, Inc. An application for a registered trademark of the "HUMANO-
MORPHS" logo and design is pending with the Federal Patent and Trademark
office.

ISBN 1-57657-339-7

EXCLUSIVE DISTRIBUTION BY PARADISE PRESS, INC.

Cover Design & Illustrations by Nicholas Forder

Printed in the U.S.A.

Prologue

I should have known that as soon as Ezra got some kind of superpower he would use it for evil.

Well, not *evil* really, but certainly not for good.

Hayden and I weren't exactly thinking we should all put on blue tights and red capes and go around saving the world, but we also didn't think Ezra's approach was all that enlightened either.

Because as soon as we got the morphing power — the power to change ourselves into any other person we wanted to — Ezra decided to change himself into Mr. Klonk, our principal at Messetup Middle School.

He was going to wait until Klonk called in sick one day, then morph himself into a perfect copy of Klonk. Then he'd spend the day as Klonk, giving grief to all the teachers.

I was tempted, too. I thought about using my morphing power to get revenge on the snotty cheerleaders who tormented me.

But I'm getting ahead of myself.

My name's Abby Moody, and Hayden and I and our friend Ezra are eighth graders at Messetup. I'd like to say we're all good-looking and popular and smart, but we're really just smart — and sometimes Hayden and I aren't too sure about Ezra.

We got this power to morph into other human beings — to be Humanomorphs, as I called us — in an accident at this factory, involving chemicals and lightning.

But there were problems, like the more we morphed the more we started getting these really weird nightmares.

And the nightmares weren't even the worst of it. 'Cause the factory we had been snooping around at had caught us on surveillance cameras, and their guards came looking for us at school.

And they found us.

It turned out the factory was making a new kind of super-poisonous spray that they planned to use on the Amazon rain forest, to clear out thousands of acres. They were afraid we'd found out their secret, and they weren't too happy. They wanted to shut us up — permanently.

2

We were just three kids (and one of us was Ezra, which counts even more against us). But we did have the power to morph.

And maybe that power would give us the ability to save the rain forest.

Chapter One

It was another typical morning at Messetup Middle School. This was back before we got the power to morph, and we had no hint of what was to come.

The cool girls were hanging around outside the entrance, checking out their perfect hair and their perfect makeup in their little makeup compact mirrors. The cool guys were trying to get the cool girls' attention by telling jokes in loud voices and punching each other in the arm.

The brainiacs were already in their classes, already at their desks, re-checking the math homework they'd done the night before and discussing what they were going to do their Science Fair projects on.

The bad kids were in the boys' bathroom, drawing on the walls of the bathroom stalls with magic markers.

Messetup Middle School is in a pretty nice,

safe suburb, but a handful of boys like to pretend they're inner-city gang members, wearing big baggy pants that hang down off their waists and backwards baseball caps. They always say "Yo!" to each other and draw graffiti on the walls.

Hayden, Ezra and I turned off the sidewalk and walked up to the steps and the big double wooden doors. Suddenly, one of the cool guys called Hayden's name.

Hayden jerked like he'd been shot by a sniper — Hayden, Ezra and I don't exactly hang out with the cool kids, or the brainiacs, or the homey-wannabes.

We don't hang with anybody, except each other. Some of the other kids probably think we're misfits, but we just have our own little clique of three.

Maybe it sounds strange, two boys and a girl just hanging out together in their own little group. But we've been neighbors and friends since third grade.

Still, when Chip George, the star of the football team, stops flirting with Amanda Walker, the blonde cheerleader, and calls you to come over, well, you have to pay attention.

So Hayden did.

He walked over to Chip and a few other of the cool guys. I watched as Chip put his arm around Hayden's shoulder and led him away from the group, talking to him in a low voice.

Strange. Very strange indeed.

Maria, one of the cheerleaders in what Ezra called "the loathsome foursome," put away her compact and looked up and saw Ezra and me.

"Look who's here, dudes," she said to her friends. That was the latest "cool" thing that the cool girls did, call each other "dude," like they were surfers in Southern California.

"If it isn't Abby Moody," Maria called loudly.

"How are you feeling today, Abby? Moody?"

Her friends all exploded into laughter at her lame joke, one I'd heard in various forms for three or four years now.

"I'd be moody too if I looked like that," said Kelly.

Hey, I thought, I don't look that bad. So my hair isn't blonde and doesn't have that perfect little wave to it. It's brown and straight and short, but OK. In fact, that's me all over: OK brown eyes, OK medium height and weight, OK figure.

Speaking of lame jokes, this is probably a good time to explain about the name of our school, Messetup Middle School. It's pronounced "Mess-ED-up," and it's an old Indian word meaning "great river." Actually, our school is named after the Messetup River that flows through town.

Just about every kid who's ever attended Messetup, though, has pronounced it "Mess It Up," or "Messed Up." It's an old joke, one that the teachers have gotten used to over the years.

But Ezra, being Ezra, had taken the joke name to new heights, or new lows, depending on how you saw it.

At a football game a month ago, he had "borrowed" one of the megaphones that the cheerleaders use to lead the crowd, and stood up in the front row of the spectator stands. He turned around, facing the crowd.

"Say it loud! Say it proud! This is one big messed up crowd!" he had yelled, imitating a cheer.

The kids had all laughed, but the grown-ups didn't think it was funny. Neither did the cheerleaders — Angela, Amanda, Maria and Kelly and the rest. They were used to being the center of attention.

"Hey ho! What do you know! We're all messed up with no place to go!" Ezra had bellowed.

At this point, Mr. Klonk, the principal, had made his way over to Ezra, and told him to put down the megaphone. Then he grasped Ezra firmly on the upper part of his arm and marched him out of the stands and back towards the concession area.

That's when he told Ezra that he was giving him detention after school every day for a week, cleaning desks.

When that week was finished, Ezra said he would never chew a piece of gum again for the rest of his life. There was nothing grosser in this world, he told us, then squatting down with a putty knife in one hand and scraping dried gum off the underside of desks.

"No, I take that back," he told Hayden and me. "There is one thing grosser than scraping dried gum off the bottom of a desk."

"What's that?" we asked. We should have known Ezra was setting us up.

"The only thing grosser than scraping dried gum off the underside of a desk is scraping off gum that hasn't completely dried yet."

"Eeeewwwww," I said, and made a face.

"Aw, come on, Abby. Here, I saved you a piece," Ezra said, and reached his hand down into his pants pocket.

I started to run away, but Ezra pulled his hand out empty.

That was Ezra.

Chapter Two

I had turned away from Amanda and Angela and their little gang of stuck-up cheerleaders, and saw Hayden walking back over to us.

"What was that all about?" I asked Hayden as he re-joined Ezra and me. "Since when is Chip your buddy?"

"Better known as Chip Off the Old Block-head," said Ezra.

"I've got some good news and some bad news," said Hayden.

"What's up?" I asked.

"Well, the good news is that Chip invited me to join this club that some of the guys have. They call themselves the Cruisers, and they get together and just hang out. Chip's one of the leaders, and Brian and Kyle and Tony are all in it, too."

"And they asked *you*?" said Ezra.

I understood his lack of understanding. Brian

and Kyle and Tony were some of the guys that had been hanging around the cheerleaders when we'd walked up. Brian was president of the eighth grade class and was going steady with Maria; she even wore his ID bracelet.

These guys were like the cream of the eighth grade. And Hayden, even though he was my best friend — well, Hayden was like the skim milk of the eighth grade.

Why would the Cruisers ask Hayden to join, when they made fun of him and Ezra and me?

"Yeah, he asked me," Hayden said. "But here's the bad news. I have to pass the initiation test."

"How bad is this bad news?" I asked.

"I don't know yet," said Hayden. "But I'll know tonight. They told me I have to sneak inside that deserted factory on the outskirts of town. I somehow have to get inside there and find something and bring it back to them."

"What do you have to find?" I asked.

"Anything, but it has to be something that could only have come from inside the factory. Like, I don't know, a sign or some paper about what the factory used to make or something."

"The factory" was what we all called the

enormous dark building that had sat, unattended, on a huge fenced-in lot for years.

We never went there, because there was nothing to do there and it wasn't on the way to anywhere else. About the only times we saw it, really, were when we were riding with our parents, driving out of town on the highway, just past the City Limits sign.

The factory was two stories high and kind of ominous looking. It had no windows and you couldn't even see a door from the road. A building with no windows at all is pretty strange.

It's as if it's trying to keep secrets.

Plus there was the fence. This wasn't any regular fence like the kind people put around their backyards to keep their dogs from getting loose, the kind that any 14-year-old with even a dab of athletic ability could climb with no trouble.

This was a fence abut ten feet high, and instead of being chain-link, like backyard fences, it was made of black metal poles, each about an inch thick, set very close together so you couldn't see in very well.

Once, a couple of years ago, I had been riding with my dad past the factory and had asked him what the building was. He said he had no idea, that it had been closed down when we moved to town. That was more than ten years ago, when I was only four years old.

"Are you gonna do it?" I asked Hayden. "Are you really going to go in the factory just to be able to join the Cruisers?"

"I'll have to think about it," Hayden said.

"Well, if you go, we'll go with you," I said boldly.

"Say what?" squeaked Ezra. "Excuse me, Abby, but did you just volunteer me for a mission at night that could be potentially dangerous, and one I get nothing out of?"

"If you don't want to go, Ezra, you don't have to," I told him. "But I thought it would be a nice supportive thing to do for Hayden, so he wouldn't have to go alone. He's our friend. And in case you haven't noticed, we're not exactly swarmed with so many friends that we lose count of them all."

Ezra looked kind of ashamed. I felt proud of myself for volunteering and being such a good friend to Hayden.

The morning bell rang and we walked up the steps and into school together, the three of us, ready to start another day at Messetup.

But as the day wore on, my bravery started

turning to a bad case of nerves.

What in the heck had I signed us up for? Maybe Ezra was being chicken, but he had a point. Hayden was doing this to get into the Cruisers, but what were Ezra and I getting out of this nighttime mission into the old abandoned factory?

If anything, we'd be the losers. Because if the Cruisers really did let Hayden join once he completed the mission, we'd probably see less of him.

He'd have new friends. Cooler friends. Ezra and I would start looking like yesterday's lunch.

Swell. What had I gotten myself into?

Chapter Three

As we walked home from school, Hayden told Ezra and me what we had already known was coming: He was going to go for the initiation into the Cruisers.

"If you guys don't want to come, I understand," he said. "But this is my big chance. If I get into the Cruisers, it opens all kinds of doors. Including the door that leads to Angela, maybe."

I was hurt, but I stayed quiet.

I knew Hayden had a crush on Angela, and that she viewed him on about the same level as she viewed the dead frog she had been forced to dissect in biology class last semester.

And it wasn't like I was jealous, was it? Well, was it? Hayden was a friend, just a friend.

But at fourteen, things sometimes feel a bit confused. I'd been noticing how tall he'd gotten in the last year, and the way his brown hair hung down along the right side of his forehead almost to his right eye, and how that was a good look on him.

Snap out of it, Abby, I told myself.

"So when are you going?" Ezra asked.

"As soon as it gets dark," Hayden answered. "I'll say I'm going over to Abby's house to study. Ezra, you say that you are, too. Abby, you say you're coming to *my* house to study. We'll meet at the school, and it's probably about a fifteen-minute walk from there to the factory. We get in, we get out, we go home. End of story."

"End of story," I repeated.

Of course, it was actually going to be the beginning of the story, not the end, but none of us knew that then.

So we went home, ate dinner with our families, gathered our book bags, and met at school.

We had to take our book bags so our parents would think we were studying. But we didn't want to take them to the factory because who knew what might happen there and we wanted to be able to travel fast if we needed to.

So we went behind the school to the football stadium (the scene of Ezra's famous cheers), and stashed our book bags under the bleachers in a dark spot where no one would find them.

Hayden had estimated the walk to the factory correctly — about fifteen minutes.

Hayden and I were quiet as we walked. I felt a little nervous.

Ezra, being Ezra, kept up a non-stop barrage of chatter. He told us this story about some teenage couple that parks at a lover's lane, and there's this maniac with a hook instead of a hand, and he kills the boy somehow and the girl drives away and when she gets to the police station the guy's hook is caught in her door handle.

Or something like that.

"Ezra, will you please shut up?" Hayden said. We were anxious enough about going into this abandoned factory at night, even without Ezra rattling on about a maniac who kills teenagers.

Thanks, Ezra. Way to be.

It didn't help that a thunderstorm appeared to be gathering force. Off in the distance we could see flashes of lightning, followed a few seconds later by a very low rumble.

The air smelled like rain.

The fence appeared on our right. Through it, we could see the hulking shell of the abandoned building.

17

A full moon shone, giving us light to see by, but the main thing we could see was that the building was very dark. The grounds surrounding it were every bit as dark.

"OK, first thing. How do we get in?" I asked Hayden. "Are we going to climb this ten-foot fence?"

"I was hoping there would be an opening or a break somewhere," he said. "Let's start following it around towards the back and look for a way in."

The lot was several acres big. We walked away from the street, and without the sound of cars, we seemed to be all alone in the world.

We peered at the fence as we walked, looking for a hole or something.

Ezra saw it first. Not a hole, not a break. A gate. A gate in the back.

It was chained and locked, but there was a gap where the gate met the fence. It was too narrow for most adults to squeeze through, but three 14-year-old kids could make it.

So in we went, one by one, squishing our bodies through the narrow passage.

Chapter Four

Once we were on the grounds, the factory loomed ahead of us. We still had no idea how we would get inside, or what Hayden could take for his initiation.

"Isn't this, like, stealing?" I asked.

"Yeah, I thought of that before and it started to bother me," Hayden said. "I don't want to steal. So I came up with a better plan. All Chip said I had to do was prove I was in the factory. So I brought this."

He reached into his jacket pocket and pulled out a small camera with a pop-up flash.

"You guys take a couple of pics of me and, boom, we're out of here," Hayden said.

"Cool," said Ezra. "Can I get my picture taken too?"

"Sure, Ez, if we have time," said Hayden.

The thunderstorm we had noticed earlier was moving closer.

The lightning was no longer an occasional, blurry glow on the horizon, but sharp streaks of light zigzagging across the dark sky. The thunder followed the lightning more closely now, meaning the storm was moving towards us.

By now we were up to the factory itself. The moon had gone behind a cloud, and it was darker than dark.

"Anybody see a door?" I whispered.

"I can't see my own hand in front of my face," Ezra said.

"Come on, guys, let's hurry this up or we're going to get wet," I said. "There's a storm coming."

We came to what appeared to be a loading dock in back of the factory. There were lots of big green barrels stacked up on their ends, piled about three barrels high. There must have been fifty of them.

Suddenly, the moon came back out and illuminated the scene.

"You know, guys, those barrels don't look ten years old," I said.

"You're right," said Hayden. "They look new. Why would there be new barrels stacked behind an abandoned factory?"

I walked over and squinted at one. There was

20

lettering on the side, and I could barely read it in the moonlight:

CAUTION!! HANDLE WITH CARE!!
Property of RF Industries, Inc.
Destination: Mato Grosso, Brazil, South
America
EXTREMELY TOXIC!

I read the wording aloud to Hayden and Ezra.

"And if that's not weird enough, guys," I told them, "this lettering is fresh. It looks like it's been spray-painted on this barrel in the past day or two."

We examined the barrels quickly. They all bore the same warning, that the contents were toxic and they were going to Brazil.

"This is a real mystery," Ezra said. "Better than the guy with the hook."

"Enough about the hook," Hayden said. "I don't get this. Everybody in town thinks this place hasn't been used for years, and here's evidence that some company has been using it recently. Very recently."

He looked at Ezra and me.

"And if these barrels are stamped with a desti-

21

nation, maybe they're going to be shipped out soon," Hayden continued. "Maybe this factory isn't really abandoned."

Needless to say, we were all getting the willies about now. I suddenly had this strong intuition that whoever had stored a bunch of barrels full of something poisonous would not want teenagers poking around them at night.

"Let's get your picture taken and get out of here, Hayden," I said. "I don't like this."

"But I've got to get inside," Hayden said.

"I think I see a window," Ezra said. He was looking up and pointing.

Sure enough, although there were no windows that could be seen from the road, there were a few up high here on the back side of the factory. The lowest one was above the stack of barrels.

"I'm going in," said Hayden.

Chapter Five

"You still want to go in, even though the factory is being used?" I asked

"Look, Abby, we've gone to all this trouble," Hayden said. "I just want to get my picture taken and then we'll leave. It's my only chance to get into the Cruisers."

"But one of us will have to go in with you to take your picture," I said.

"I'll go," said Ezra. He was very unpredictable. Afraid one moment, courageous the next.

Ezra didn't even wait to hear any more of my objections to what I thought was becoming a very dangerous game. He started climbing onto the barrels.

Ezra was small and light for his age, and moved quickly, picking his way up onto the stacked barrels like a sure-footed billy goat climbing a mountain. In only a few seconds, he had reached the top.

23

The window was only an arm's reach away.

That's when it happened, and it happened so fast Hayden and I didn't even have time for it to register.

Suddenly the barrels started moving. The bottom ones began wobbling, then the middle ones, then the ones on top where Ezra was standing. In a couple of seconds, barrels were flying everywhere. Ezra was falling.

"*Hellllpppppp!*" he yelled.

We didn't see the barrel that broke open. Maybe the top was loose, or maybe Ezra, while kicking and flailing in his panic, knocked the top off somehow.

It must have been one of the barrels that was stacked up on top, because suddenly Hayden and I were drenched in some awful liquid.

It smelled like the pesticide my dad put out on the weeds in his garden. Only about a hundred times stronger than that.

Ezra came tumbling towards us, right through the thick wave of goo that was flying out of the barrel. He landed on top of Hayden, and the two boys fell to the ground.

This is awful, I thought. This is the worst that

could happen.

I was wrong.

Just then, a bolt of lightning speared out of the sky. It crackled to earth and seemed to hit in the woods behind the factory. It was so close that it lit up everything around us as if it was noon on a sunny day at the beach.

In the split-second of bright light, I saw Hayden and Ezra lying on the ground. They were soaking with the poisonous stuff from inside the barrel that had broken open.

I could feel that I was soaking wet with the same horrible stuff.

At almost at the same instant the lightning hit, the thunder roared. The storm was upon us.

"Come on guys, let's get out of here!" I yelled.

"My initiation! My picture!" Hayden hollered back.

"You idiot! We've been drenched with something labeled toxic and we're in the middle of a lightning storm!" I screamed. "We're in danger of dying right now, and even if we survive the lightning, we may be poisoned and get some hideous disease!"

They didn't need any more persuading. All three of us took off running back towards the gate.

The lightning flashed around us. Then the rain started to fall. Thick, heavy drops — so many of them that it was like being inside a car wash.

Normally I don't like being out in the rain, but it flashed through my mind that maybe this was the best thing that could happen, that the rain would wash off all this poisonous goop that covered us. That had to be good.

We reached the big iron gate — Ezra first, then Hayden, then me. We were all in a panic, and people don't always behave well in a panic.

Ezra was squeezing through the opening, and was halfway through with the gate pressed against his chest and the fence pressed against his back. Hayden was pushing him, yelling at him to hurry.

I had somehow grabbed Hayden's hand and was holding on to it tightly.

Don't try to make anything out of me holding Hayden's hand. It wasn't the way a couple hold hands when they're going together. I was so scared at that point I probably would have held the hand of Frankenstein.

And that's when lightning hit the fence.

Chapter Six

I'd never been hit by lightning before.

I'd read newspaper stories about people who had been struck and who had lived, and people who had been hit and died.

I was one of the lucky ones. So were Ezra and Hayden.

We didn't actually see the bolt that hit us. One moment we were all pushing up against the iron gate and then the next moment there was this explosion.

That's the only way to describe it.

And then we were all sitting on the ground. My ears were ringing. I smelled something nasty, like burning hair.

I looked at Hayden and Ezra, and they were sitting down, kind of stunned.

They didn't know what had hit them. Actually, none of us did right at that moment. It was only later, in talking about it, that we figured out we'd been struck by lightning.

The lightning had treated the gate worse than us. It was pretty much blown right off its hinges. Now, instead of a gate, there was an opening big enough to drive a truck through. (Little did we know at that time that was exactly RF Industries' plan — to drive a truck through the gate to pick up the mystery barrels.)

We picked ourselves up slowly. Nobody said a word. It was probably just as well, because my ears were ringing so loudly that I couldn't have heard what they said anyway.

We started to run, through the open gate, back out to the road, and back towards the school. We grabbed our book bags from their hiding place — fortunately the bleachers had sheltered them and they didn't get wet — and headed for our homes.

Ezra's parents weren't home, so we went to his house. By the time we got there, we were exhausted, gasping for breath from our long run, soaking wet from the rain, and still reeking of the chemicals that had been dumped on us.

"Man, I hope you're happy!" I snapped at Hayden.

"I'm sorry!" he pleaded. "I didn't know . . ."

I started to catch my breath and calm down.

"Nobody could have known. I'm sorry you didn't get your picture."

"That's OK. I'm just happy to be alive."

Ezra was quiet. No cheers, no hook-man stories, no nothing.

The next hour or so passed in kind of a blur. We stripped off our wet clothes. I got in the shower, and borrowed Ezra's dad's bathrobe when I got out.

Ezra had put all our wet, stinking clothes into the dryer. He really should have put them through the washer first, but we didn't have time.

When they were dry, Hayden and I got into our clothes. They didn't smell that bad considering what they had been through.

I walked home, only about five houses down from Ezra, and said hey to my mom and dad, who were in the den watching TV.

Mom asked if I'd gotten caught in the storm, and I said no. She looked and saw that my clothes were dry.

I went upstairs, stripped, put on my pajamas, and dropped into bed. I was more tired than I had ever been in my life, but at least my heartbeat was back to something like normal.

In the middle of the night, I woke up feeling

funny. It was a really odd feeling, like my body was all tingling. Like it wanted to go someplace and I wasn't keeping up with it.

I took a sip of water from my nightstand and tried to go back to sleep, but I couldn't.

My face was tingling the most of all. It felt like someone was poking me with little pins — not hard, mean pokes but tiny little gentle pokes, all at once, thousands of them on every square inch of skin.

I got up to go to the bathroom that's connected by a door to my bedroom. As I walked past the mirror, I turned on the bathroom light. What I saw totally freaked me out.

I looked just like my mother!

I mean, I *was* my mother. I had changed into her!

I had gained about forty pounds, and my pajamas were unbelievably tight, bulging at the seams. My face looked forty years old, because it was my mother's forty-year-old face.

And without makeup. Man, talk about scary!

I stared at my reflection in the mirror. What had happened to me?

Chapter Seven

The bathroom light was harsh on my skin. My heart was racing again. How had I changed into my mother?

I started gasping for air. I bent down and turned on the cold water, then scooped big handfuls of cold water onto my forty-year-old face.

And that's when I woke up.

Holy Oil of Olay! I thought. It was a dream. A really intense dream. I was still in my bed, in the dark.

I jumped up. I had to be sure.

I ran into the bathroom and hit the light switch. I looked in the mirror. It was me, Abby Moody, age fourteen, an eighth grader at Messetup Middle School. Short brown hair, and all.

Not forty-year-old Eleanor Moody. As much as I loved her, I really didn't want to turn into my mom.

Just a dream.

I went back to bed, fell back to sleep, and did not dream again that night.

The next morning, Hayden and Ezra and I met up a few blocks from school. We agreed that we wouldn't tell anybody the details of what had happened last night.

Either they wouldn't believe us, or they'd turn it into some way to make fun of us, getting doused with chemicals and struck by lightning.

"I don't know what I'll tell Chip," Hayden lamented. "I guess I won't get into the Cruisers now."

"Hey, why do they call themselves the Cruisers?" Ezra asked. "Cruising means driving around, and none of these guys are old enough to even have a learner's permit. I think the only cruising they do is in their heads."

"I don't know, and it doesn't look like I'll find out," Hayden said. He hung his head. The poor guy was really dejected.

As we approached the steps leading up to the school door, the usual gang was holding court. Today was a pep rally, so Amanda, Angela, Kelly and Maria were all wearing their cheerleading costumes.

I noticed Hayden perked up a little when he saw them, which didn't do *my* spirits any good.

"Hey, dudes, look what the cat dragged in," said Kelly, and the others tittered.

"If it isn't the Three Stooges, or two stooges and a stooge-ette," cracked Amanda, looking at me.

My face felt hot with shame.

"Hey-hey Hayden," called Maria. "Did you accomplish your mission last night?"

Obviously Chip and the Cruisers had been sharing their plans with the girls. I didn't think the guys really had any intention of letting Hayden in; I think they just wanted to find a new way to humiliate him.

If he had successfully brought back proof that he had been inside the factory, they'd have made up reasons why they didn't believe him, and maybe sent him out for another "initiation."

We walked past our tormentors and into the school. I was still troubled by the way Hayden had paid more attention to the cute girls than to me. I made a quick stop in the girls' rest room before my first class.

"Darn it all," I was thinking. "I hate those girls, but there's a little part of me that wishes I was like them. Everybody would think I was so cool, and the boys would pay more attention to me. I wish I was more like Maria."

Suddenly I felt my body start to tingle. It was the same tingling feeling I had had last night in my weird dream, but this was no dream. I was wide awake, and in the middle school bathroom.

I rushed to the big mirror above the sinks.

My short brown hair was changing color, getting lighter, blonder. And it was getting longer and thicker. My facial features were shifting, like some special effect in a monster movie.

I couldn't believe my eyes. I was morphing into Maria!

Not just my face, but my body was changing, too. I felt like I was growing a couple of inches. My ankles were suddenly sticking out of the bottom of my blue jeans. My long-sleeved shirt cuffs didn't come all the way down to my wrists. My arms and legs were growing.

Within a matter of seconds, it was no longer Abby Moody looking back at me from the bathroom mirror. It was Maria Hill, nasty but popular cheerleader.

My brown eyes were blue; my nose was shorter and a little turned up at the end; my hair was blonde and lustrous, like some model in a shampoo commercial.

I had morphed into my worst enemy.

"Maybe it's a dream, maybe it's a dream," I kept telling myself.

But it was no dream this time.

Chapter Eight

What the heck was I going to do?

I couldn't go to class this way. Would I go to Abby Moody's classes or Maria Hill's?

If I went to Maria's there would be two of us. If I went to my own classes, I'd be marked absent, and the teacher would ask Maria why she was in the wrong class.

And what about after school? Could I just go home and say hey to my parents and tell them, "Oh, by the way, I grew two inches in twelve hours and completely changed my bone structure and my speaking voice, but really, it's me, Abby, under this skin."

Even worse, anyone could walk into the bathroom at any minute and think I was Maria and start talking to me. What if my voice wasn't hers?

"Testing, one, two, three," I said.

My voice was Maria's, not my own. Even though my mind was reeling, I figured that if my body had somehow morphed into Maria Hill's, my vocal cords would be hers as well, since they were a part of her body.

But my mind, I realized, was still my own. I was Abby Moody's brain trapped inside Maria's body.

I had to think fast. What had caused this?

Of course, stupid. The accident last night. I'd been doused with some unknown chemical, then struck by lightning, and within a matter of hours my body had changed.

It all made sense, in a scary, weird, science-fiction kind of way.

But why had I changed into *Maria*?

Duh! Because I had wished to be like her!

So maybe, just maybe, if I wished to be Abby, I would change back into Abby. It wasn't much of a plan, but it was better than going around as Maria all day.

"I wish I was Abby Moody," I said out loud, in Maria's voice.

Again, I felt the tingling all over. And, even faster this time, I started to change back into Abby.

It was like watching the process that had happened two minutes ago, only being rewound on a VCR. And, *boom*, just like that, I was Abby again.

School was a blur for the rest of the day.

During math, I wondered if this was a condition I could control, or if it would just pop up at random, maybe in public. During English, I wondered if Hayden and Ezra had the same situation, since they'd been through the same accident.

While Mr. Ingles, my social studies teacher, droned on about the geography of South America, I worried whether this condition was permanent or not.

"Mato Grosso, Miss Moody. Miss Moody? *Hello?*"

It was Mr. Ingles, breaking into my thoughts.

"I'm sorry, what was the question?" I asked.

"Mato Grosso. Where is it?" he asked again.

"I'm sorry. I don't know."

"Well, for your information, it's a large region in Brazil, as well as a city found in that region. The area is known for its thousands of square miles of beautiful and dense tropical rain forests. As we have been studying, the Amazon rain forests are crucial to sustaining life on earth. The trees there pump out vast quantities of oxygen, which maintains the quality of the atmosphere worldwide. Without the rain forests, some scientists believe, life could become extinct on this planet."

"Mato Grosso," I thought. "That sounds so familiar. Where have I seen that name?"

But I soon started obsessing again about this morphing thing, and forgot all about Mato Grosso.

Which only goes to show, I guess, that sometimes you should pay attention in social studies class.

Chapter Nine

I couldn't wait until school was out and I could talk to Ezra and Hayden.

But I wanted to wait until we were somewhere safe. Knowing Ezra, if I told him about the morphing thing while we were walking home, he'd try it himself right there on the sidewalk.

And if he had the power, he'd change into another person right out in public, where everyone could see.

I wasn't sure exactly why, but that didn't sound like a good idea. We needed to keep this secret until we figured out what was going on.

So there we were, the three of us, finally, in my garage. I told them about my dream the night before, and then about changing into Maria in the girls' bathroom, and changing back into myself.

Hayden and Ezra looked at me like I was insane.

"I think the lightning has scrambled your brains, Abby," said Hayden.

"More like fried," said Ezra. "Sunny side up. This is your brain. This is your brain on lightning."

"It happened, guys, it really did," I insisted. "And since you two had exactly the same experience as me, you may have the same condition. Try it."

"OK, said Ezra. "I wish I was, uhhh, I don't know. Who should I wish for?"

"Michael Jordan," said Hayden.

But as soon as Hayden said the name, *he* started morphing.

He shot up in height, and his skin changed from pink to brown. His hair disappeared, and within a couple of seconds he was completely bald. An earring appeared on his left earlobe.

Hayden had become Michael Jordan!

His clothes looked ridiculous — a fourteen-year-old boy's clothes on a huge man. His shirt had split open and was in tatters. His pants clung to him, just barely, but his bare legs, heavy and muscular, stuck out almost a foot below his cuffs.

"Oww, my feet!" was all Hayden could say.

His feet had expanded within their shoes, which now pinched him. He bent over and quickly unlaced his sneakers.

Ezra didn't take long to want to play.

"I wanna be Dennis Rodman!" he shouted.

Instantly, the same transformation process occurred. Only in addition to becoming tall, black and muscular, Ezra now had wild tattoos all over his body. His hair was bright orange.

"It works! Wow! I can't believe it!" they both started yelling at once.

"Quiet, you guys," I said.

I explained to them that I was worried, and I thought this had to remain secret until we figured out what was going on.

If anybody found out, including our parents, we'd probably be whisked off to some hospital or medical lab, where we'd be studied like lab specimens. Our schoolmates, who weren't exactly kind to us right now, would label us freaks — and rightly so.

We *were* freaks! Here I was, Abby Moody, standing in my garage, with Michael Jordan and Dennis Rodman.

We had acquired the power to morph into other humans. We were some kind of Humanomorphs.

"Hey, let's go shoot some hoops!" said Ezra.

"No, you idiots," I said, and I had to explain all over again.

This time they understood.

Ezra was particularly disappointed he couldn't go back to his house and practice slam-dunks on the basketball hoop in his driveway, or walk over to school and sign autographs.

But he and Hayden understood my point about keeping this new power a secret.

"Hey Abby, I have an idea," said Ezra. "Why don't you morph into Cindy Crawford."

I glared at him. I knew he wasn't really interested in seeing my morphing power. He just liked the idea of hanging around with Cindy Crawford.

And I must admit, there was a small part of me that was tempted.

But I resisted.

"Get back to yourselves, guys," I told them. "Come on. You've got to get home and hide those shirts you've, uh, outgrown."

Reluctantly, they agreed, and morphed back into themselves. Now we were just Abby, Hayden and Ezra again. Somehow it didn't seem as exciting as being Cindy Crawford, Michael Jordan and Dennis Rodman.

But somehow, it felt safer. As if maybe we had been playing with something we shouldn't be playing with.

The rest of the afternoon and night seemed terrifically boring. Homework, dinner, dishes, more homework.

I called Hayden on the phone, but we were awkward, not knowing whether to talk about the morphing, or what to say.

In the middle of the night, I woke up again, feeling the same tingling that signaled a morph.

Another nightmare, or a real morph? I didn't know.

I went into the bathroom, turned on the light, looked in the mirror.

Looking back at me was the face of Ezra.

Chapter Ten

"Oh please, oh please, oh please," I said to myself, "let this be a dream."

It was Ezra's voice talking.

This was creeping me out big time.

BRRRRRINNNNNNGGGGG went my alarm, and I woke up. As Abby Moody, in my own bed. I didn't even have to look in the mirror, I knew I was me.

But I also knew that the morphing nightmares were no fun at all.

I had no idea how this power worked. Since all I had to do was think about somebody to become him or her in real life, what if I dreamed I was somebody and became them in real life and not just in my dream?

Did that make sense? If it didn't, that was OK, because nothing else did, either.

At school, I concentrated on not wanting to be anybody else.

It was hard. If someone tells you over and over, "Don't think of a blue elephant, don't think of a blue elephant," sooner or later you're going to think of a blue elephant.

The last thing I wanted to turn into in the middle of class was a blue elephant. Or Angela. Or Cindy Crawford. Or anybody.

Frankly, I was really starting to hate this morphing power. The potential for public humiliation was just too great.

On the walk home that afternoon, Hayden and Ezra and I compared notes. Hayden was having the same feelings I was. He wanted to morph into a movie star, or the President of the United States, but he realized there were so many drawbacks. The clothes wouldn't fit right. Maybe he would be discovered and taken away somewhere for experimentation.

I was glad Hayden and I were on the same wavelength.

Ezra, however, was on his own wavelength. Radio Ezra, we sometimes called it — his own little signal that only he can hear.

As we walked, he told us about his day.

He had passed the school office in the morning, and he had overheard one of the secretaries say that Principal Klonk had called in sick that day.

That had given him a very Ezra-ish idea.

He left school and went outside, strolling non-chalantly until he was outside the principal's window. He peeped in through the blinds.

The office was empty, the lights off. Sure enough, no Klonk.

Ezra tried the window. It was unlocked. Who was going to have the guts to sneak into the principal's office through the window?

Hayden and I knew who would have the guts, or the stupidity.

Quickly, our buddy had climbed inside the office. He had shown at least a glimmer of intelligence, and realized he would need adult clothes.

Klonk had a large bureau in one corner of his office, which Ezra had seen on one of his trips to the office for a discussion of what Klonk called Ezra's "attitude problem."

Ezra opened the bureau and presto! change-o!

There was a spare suit, shirt and tie that Klonk kept, apparently in case of emergency. Maybe he'd need it if some kid spilled Coke all over him in the cafeteria and he had a meeting with the school board in the afternoon.

Ezra locked Klonk's office door from the inside, stripped down to his underwear and put on Klonk's clothes.

I had to hand it to the boy, considering he was doing something extremely stupid and dangerous, he was showing some good planning.

Then Ezra morphed into Principal Klonk. He looked in the mirror, and he *was* Klonk. He spoke a few test words, and Klonk's voice came out.

He unlocked the office door, and stepped into the outer office.

Ms. Frost, Klonk's secretary, about had a heart attack, Ezra told us.

"Mr. Klonk sir," she stammered. "I, I, I thought you weren't coming in. I didn't see you come in."

"Oh, well, I got to feeling better and thought I'd come in," The Ezra-Klonk person told her. "You must have stepped away from your desk when I walked by."

"You have several appointments today, sir," Ms. Frost told him.

"Cancel them, Ms. Frost," Ezra said. "I have several matters that need my immediate attention. Please bring me the permanent student record of Ezra

Parker. He's in eighth grade."

Hayden and I were stupefied as Ezra continued his story.

Once he had his own student record, Ezra locked his office door, or *Klonk's* office door, and went through the file carefully.

He took out several pages of disciplinary actions and records of detentions — not everything, he told us, because that would have been suspicious. Just enough to make it look better.

He changed a few grades, but only a few, he said. No one was going to believe he was suddenly a straight-A student.

Ezra pushed the red button on the intercom on his desk, the way he had seen Klonk do it.

"Ms. Frost," he said, "please send for Mr. Grossman. I want to see him immediately."

"He's teaching gym," Ms. Frost replied.

"I said I want to see him immediately," Ezra said, raising his voice. "Get him out of class."

A few minutes later, Mr. Grossman appeared in his T-shirt and shorts, with his whistle still around his neck.

Mr. Grossman and Ezra had a long-running feud, with Ezra always on the losing end. Ezra would say something smart-alecky, and Mr. Grossman would order him to do twenty push-ups.

Then Ezra would make belching noises while he did the push-ups, and Mr. Grossman would order him to do ten laps around the gym.

And on and on it went.

Well, Ezra gave poor Mr. Grossman quite the lecture that morning. He told the gym teacher to quit picking on Ezra Parker, and that young Parker was a particular favorite of Mr. Klonk's. He said he was going to ask Ezra to report back to him if Mr. Grossman was mean to him.

And he told Mr. Grossman that if he didn't follow these instructions, he might find himself looking for another job.

The gym teacher was dumbfounded. He nodded silently and walked away.

Ezra was alone in Klonk's office, wondering what to do next, when he heard Ms. Frost's voice.

"Why Mr. Klonk! What are you doing here? I thought you were inside your office."

It was the real Klonk!

And he was heading for Ezra. Klonk was about to come face to face with his exact clone, and Ezra was trapped.

Chapter Eleven

"What happened? What happened?" I shrieked at Ezra as we walked home.

"I ducked into his bathroom," Ezra said.

"He has his own bathroom in there?" Hayden asked.

"Yeah, sure," said Ezra. "He's the principal."

Ezra knew that it was a gamble, that Klonk might have to use the bathroom, but he also knew he couldn't stay sitting there at Klonk's desk.

Fortunately, he'd left his Ezra clothes on the bathroom floor. Even more fortunately, Klonk stayed in his office only a few minutes, then left.

Ezra heard the office door shut. Then he flew out of the bathroom clutching his clothes, and practically jumped out the window.

He jogged, as Klonk, to the boy's bathroom, and locked himself into a stall. Then he morphed back into Ezra. He stepped out of Klonk's suit, leaving it in a pile on the floor, and put on his own clothes.

For the rest of his career at Messetup Middle School, Mr. Klonk would wonder how his suit, shirt and tie had gotten from his bureau into the boys' bathroom.

And he also wondered why Mr. Grossman acted so strange around him.

"That's exactly the kind of stuff I'm worried about," I told Ezra. I was glad to see Hayden nodding in agreement. We had both enjoyed the story thoroughly, and even had a bit of admiration for Ezra's cleverness.

"Nothing happened," Ezra said. "I got away with it."

"But what if you had gotten caught?" Hayden asked. "How would you have explained it? Once they had your parents in there, and maybe some cops, and maybe a psychiatrist, and they're all pressuring you, how long could you last before you broke down and told them about me and Abby and what happened at the factory?"

Ezra didn't have an answer. He seemed shocked that his friends had turned on him instead of appreciating his great adventure.

"Plus, Ezra, we don't know how this works," I

said. "What if you morph into someone and you get stuck?"

"You sound like my mom," Ezra said. "When I was little I used to practice crossing my eyes, and she'd tell me if I did that they might get stuck that way."

"Well, that's just mom-talk," I said. "We're dealing with something here we don't understand. You think I'm not tempted to morph into one of my favorite TV stars, or somebody cool just to see what it's like? But we don't understand this process. What if the morphing power suddenly wears off while I'm someone else?

"Then Abby Moody would cease to exist."

Whoa. As soon as I said it, I realized I hadn't even thought it through that far. The more you thought about it, the scarier this morphing power was.

Chapter Twelve

That night, I had no nightmares. Thank goodness. I was scared enough of reality.

And reality was about to get a lot scarier.

It was another typical day at Messetup Middle School. Cool kids hung out on the steps, full of hot air and their own self-importance.

Bad boys hung out in the bathroom, spreading the bizarre rumor about the kid who'd found the principal's clothes the day before.

Brainiacs sat in their seats like good little brainiacs, blah, blah, blah.

During third period, my life changed. Again.

The intercom squawked to life: "Abby Moody, please report to the principal's office. Abby Moody, principal's office."

I had never been called to Klonk's office. Was this in connection with Ezra's prank? It had to be.

I got up slowly and walked to Klonk's office.

Ms. Frost showed me inside.

Klonk was seated behind his desk. Standing next to him was a tall man. He was dressed like a funeral director — black suit, black shoes, white shirt, dark tie. His hair was short and neatly trimmed. He wore a very serious expression.

"Miss Moody," said Mr. Klonk, "this is Special Agent Burke of the Federal Bureau of Investigation. Please sit down."

The *FBI*? Holy smokes and good gadzooks, the *FBI*!

Why were they calling *me* in instead of Ezra? He was the one who had impersonated the principal.

I sat.

Burke started talking.

"Miss Moody," he said. "On the outskirts of this city there is an abandoned factory. At least most people think it is an abandoned factory. Actually, it is a top-secret plant, owned and operated by the Department of Defense. Now, what they are doing there is none of your concern. But my concern is this: Have you been there recently?"

I was stunned. What should I say? A secret Department of Defense plant?

"Miss Moody?" prompted Principal Klonk.

"Uh, uh, what makes you think I was there?" I asked, stalling for time.

"Surveillance cameras," said the FBI agent. "We have installed very small video cameras on top of some of the fence posts to keep a record of anyone who tries to breach security. Three nights ago, three teenagers broke into the grounds through a gate. We are unable to identify two of the teenagers because the camera couldn't quite get their faces. But we were able to identify the third person, Miss Moody — or rather your principal was able to when we showed him the picture."

I held my breath and waited. Then the FBI man continued.

"It was you."

I was caught. Nailed. No way out.

"I'm sorry," I blurted out. "It was me. We didn't even go inside the factory, we were just messing around, I swear."

"I think it's time I called Miss Moody's parents and had them come in," said Principal Klonk.

"That won't be necessary," said Agent Burke. "I'll take Miss Moody down to the police station, and we'll call her parents from there."

The *police* station? Oh, my gosh, this was beyond awful, beyond disaster! What was I going to do?

"Excuse me, Agent Burke," said Principal Klonk, "but that's highly irregular. This girl is a student here; she's only fourteen years old. While I understand the gravity of what she has done, I don't think it's necessary to take her to the police."

All right! Klonk to the rescue! Go Klonk!

Having my parents called in suddenly seemed not too bad an option, compared to being hauled down to the police station.

"The police are working with us," Burke replied. He seemed to be getting tense. "And your involvement with this is now over. This is official government business. Come along, young lady."

Burke stepped towards me and pulled me out of my seat.

"Now see here," said Klonk. "You can't yank a student at my school around like that."

I couldn't believe this. Klonk and the FBI agent were arguing!

"We're done here," said Burke quickly. He turned to Klonk: "I advise you to forget this matter happened." And holding my arm, he marched me out the door.

"I'm calling your superior!" Klonk shouted.

"I wouldn't advise that," Burke answered grimly on his way out the door. By now we were moving past Ms. Frost's desk.

We were walking down the hall towards the school exit when Burke's cell phone rang. He plucked it out of his jacket pocket.

"Wallace here," he answered. He kept his grip on my arm.

Wallace? I thought his name was Burke. Was one his first name and the other his last? Or was his real name Wallace?

"Yes sir, I have one of them," Burke/Wallace said into the phone. "We'll be there shortly. The pre-arranged spot."

In an instant, it all fell into place in my head.

This guy wasn't a real FBI agent. He had faked being one to fool Mr. Klonk. Maybe he even had shown him a fake badge, for all I knew.

But the real FBI wouldn't just yank a kid out of school over the principal's protest. They would re-assure the principal.

Now he said his name was Wallace, not Burke. And instead of saying he was taking me to the police station, he was taking me to some "pre-arranged spot."

He didn't work for the FBI. He worked for whoever was making toxic chemicals at the factory. What he was doing wasn't part of law enforcement. It wasn't even legal.

He was kidnapping me!

Chapter Thirteen

If I could just get away, I thought, I could go home and confess everything to my parents — the trip to the factory, the accident, the morphing.

They could call the FBI and see if there really was an Agent Burke. If there was, and I was in trouble, I'd have my parents with me instead of being alone with a guy who might be an FBI agent, or who might be working for . . . well, I didn't know, and I didn't want to find out.

I had to get away. I had to morph.

"Excuse me, please, sir," I said in a whiny voice. "I really, really have to go to the bathroom."

"You can go at the station," he growled.

"Please, sir," I said. I couldn't give up. I saw the girls' bathroom coming up on our left. "I'll just be a minute."

"You're coming with me, kid," he said. He was being a lot meaner now than when he had been with Mr. Klonk. A regular meanie.

The bathroom door was beside me. I jerked my arm hard, and it popped out of his grasp. I turned and ran into the bathroom.

I was counting on one thing. This was a school, and class was in session. Students and teachers came and went in the halls.

No way would this guy, whoever he was, risk barging into the girls' bathroom.

If he was a real FBI agent, he'd wait, knowing there was no place for me to go but out the same door I'd just gone in.

If he wasn't an FBI agent, he still couldn't risk having anyone seeing a grown man go into the girls' bathroom.

Pretty clever, Abby. Except that now I was trapped in the girls' bathroom, with Mr. Meanie right outside waiting for me.

I ducked into a stall and locked the door.

What teacher was about my size? I had to morph into somebody my size so the clothes would fit, and it had to be a teacher, because he would believe an adult more than another kid.

Miss Jensen! Math. She was about five-foot-three, my size, and about a hundred and ten pounds, about my weight.

I willed myself to become Miss Jensen, and instantly felt the tingling that signaled a morph coming on. My body changed, became more womanly, but stayed the right size within my clothes.

I unslung the book bag I'd been carrying the whole time and pulled out the navy blue pullover sweater my mom always made me carry in case it suddenly got cold for no reason.

Chalk one up for mom's paranoia about the weather!

I slipped out of my long-sleeved shirt. Underneath I was wearing a "Dawson's Creek" T-shirt. I pulled the sweater on over the T-shirt, and stashed my book bag behind the toilet, out of sight. I'd have to come back for it later.

I looked in the mirror. I was Miss Jensen — about thirty years old, with long black hair. The sweater helped me look different. Maybe Mr. Meanie wouldn't notice the jeans and Nikes were the same.

It was time for the ultimate test.

I stepped out of the bathroom. Meanie was standing right there.

"Excuse me, may I help you?" I asked in Miss Jensen's voice.

"Special Agent Burke with the FBI, ma'am," he said. I'd fooled him!

He reached into his jacket pocket, pulled out a piece of folded leather that looked like a wallet and flipped it open. I caught a glimpse of an identification card and a badge. But then he flipped it closed and put it back in his pocket.

Maybe that's the way real FBI agents showed their ID. Or maybe he didn't want people to look too closely.

"I'm escorting a female student, Abby Moody, on FBI business," he said. "Did you see her in there?"

"Yes, Abby came in while I was in there," I lied. "She said to tell you she was sorry, and she'd be right out."

That seemed to reassure him, and I walked away. I had outsmarted a kidnapper! With a little morphing help, of course.

What to do now, I wondered.

I had to warn Hayden and Ezra. Even though Mr. Meanie had said I was the only one he could identify, I had a feeling he was a liar.

Maybe he would go after one of the others next.

Since I was a teacher, I could walk around

63

Messetup Middle School freely. Well, I could walk anywhere except into Miss Jensen's class.

That would freak her out, to see me walk in as her.

I knew Hayden had math third period and Ezra had gym. I went to Hayden's math class, opened the door, and bold as you please, said to his teacher, "Excuse me a moment, I need to have a word with Hayden."

It worked. Hey, I was a teacher. Why wouldn't it work? His teacher excused him and Hayden came out into the hall.

"It's me, Abby," I whispered.

"Huh?" was all Hayden could manage. He didn't get it.

"I'm not Miss Jensen," I whispered. "I'm Abby. There's trouble. We need to get Ezra and talk."

Finally, Hayden understood. We walked quickly to gym class, where I sprung Ezra free with no problem. Mr. Grossman was being very respectful towards Ezra these days. He even called him Mr. Parker.

We hurried out an exit onto the school grounds.

"I thought we weren't supposed to morph," Ezra said, confused.

"This was different," I said "This was an emergency. But I really want to change back. If someone sees me, they'll think I'm Miss Jensen and ask me why I'm not teaching my class."

There wasn't any place really private for me to morph out in the parking lot, but there was a big tree over to one side. I made for the tree, with Hayden and Ezra following.

"You guys get on either side of me to block anybody's view," I instructed them.

I got behind the tree, and my two best friends flanked me. I quickly morphed back into myself.

We walked back to the parking lot. I was starting to tell them that I thought it was time we told our parents what had happened. We needed real help now.

We didn't notice the dark blue van with the smoked windows that pulled up silently nearby.

"I think I was almost kidnapped," I told them.

"By who?" asked Hayden.

"By me," said Mr. Meanie. The door of the van had opened. Wallace/Burke/Mr. Meanie was sitting in the passenger seat. Another guy who looked just like him was driving.

The "FBI agent" was pointing a gun right at us.

"Game's over, kids," he said. I had thought his voice was mean before, but now it was downright cruel.

"Get in the van," he growled. "Now."

Chapter Fourteen

We had no choice. The gun was pointed right at us. The tone of Mr. Meanie's voice told me he was ready to use it.

We got in the van.

"Boys on the outside, girlie in the middle," Mr. Meanie said.

We scrunched into the back seat. He hopped out, slid the door closed, and locked it. The driver pulled out of the school parking lot.

"How did you do that back in the bathroom, Miss Moody?" he asked.

Instinctively, I knew it would be a very bad idea to tell him about the morphing. We were going to have to try to escape, and being Humanomorphs might be our only way out. If they knew about it, they'd be watching for it.

I answered his question with a question of my own.

"Where are you taking us?" I asked.

We all three knew. The factory. It had to be.

The driver spoke up. "She never answered you, Wallace."

So his name *was* Wallace, not Burke. And he definitely *wasn't* an FBI agent.

"Yeah," said Wallace. "How did you get out of that bathroom?"

"Through a window," I told him. "I climbed out."

I figured Wallace didn't know if there were windows in the girls' bathroom or not. He'd have to accept my bluff.

"Our parents are going to come looking for us," Ezra spoke up. "You're gonna get busted for kidnapping."

Swell, Ezra, I thought. Get him all mad.

"*You're* gonna get busted, kid. Busted in the mouth. Shut up."

We were driving down the highway towards the factory. On foot, it had taken us fifteen minutes. In the van, it took less than five.

We took a road off the highway before we got to the factory, and drove around towards the back. Behind the factory, we saw that the gate that had been blasted off by lighting had been fixed. And now a guard stood duty.

He waved the van through the open gate. We parked in back, not far from where the barrels were stacked.

I glanced out the window and saw they had been re-piled. Not only that, but there were more of them. There must have been way over a hundred barrels now.

Whatever their concerns about us violating the factory's security, they were still making the poisonous chemicals.

"Everybody out," said Wallace. He had the gun aimed at us as he marched us up to the building.

What had appeared to us in the dark to have been a blank wall turned out to contain a camouflaged door. There was no knob, just a slot, but you could see the outline of the door.

The driver pulled out what looked like a credit card, slid it in, and the door opened.

We were inside the factory.

I had kind of hoped we'd be able to tell what the big mystery was. Maybe we would see the chemicals being made. Or maybe there would be a big sign explaining what they were for, I thought.

Duh, Abby.

But we found ourselves in a plain hall. Soon Wallace had marched us into a plain room with a wooden table and several chairs and nothing else.

"Sit," he said, as if we were dogs. But he had the gun. We sat.

The driver pulled out a walkie-talkie, thumbed a button, and spoke. "We have the three in Room A, sir."

There was a crackling response, but I couldn't quite understand it.

In a couple of minutes, a third man walked in. He was obviously the boss of Wallace and the driver, and maybe of the whole operation.

He wore a white lab coat, gold wire-rimmed glasses, and his dark hair was cut close. His eyes looked cold behind the lenses.

"Wallace, Shawn," he said to the two men. "Stick around. But I'll take it from here."

"Welcome," he said to us, but you could tell he didn't mean it. "You must be Miss Moody," he said to me. "And you two," he said to the boys, "please tell me your names."

Ezra and Hayden were trembling, they were so afraid. They didn't know what to say.

"Tell me your names immediately!" the man shouted.

"Ezra Parker," Ezra squeaked. "And what's yours?"

Good ol' Ezra. Dumb ol' Ezra. This wasn't a guy we wanted to antagonize.

"My name isn't important," he said. "But you can call me Mr. Frank."

"I'm Hayden Manchester," said Hayden.

"And what were you doing at my factory three nights ago, Mr. Manchester? The truth, please. And I have a great deal of it on videotape, so don't upset me by lying."

So Hayden told Mr. Manchester the story about the Cruisers' initiation, and how we'd squeezed through the gate. He told about Ezra climbing the barrels, the chemicals spilling, and how we ran away.

He mentioned the lightning in passing. But he didn't mention the morphing. Smart boy. Way to go, Hayden.

Mr. Frank was quiet for a few moments, lost in thought.

"What am I going to do with you three?" he said finally. It wasn't a question he wanted answered. He was just thinking out loud.

"If I let you go, you'll go straight to the police and tell them everything," he mused to himself. "If I kill you, there's going to be a lot of problems covering it up."

If he *killed* us? This was an option for this guy? Let us go or kill us?

I had to speak up, but my voice felt very tiny.

"Please, sir. We didn't really see anything. We're just kids. We don't know what's going on. There's no reason to kill us."

"Yeah, she's right," Ezra and Hayden chimed in.

"Life gets so complicated," Mr. Frank said with a sigh.

"Shawn, Wallace," he snapped to the two men. "Go get some rope and tie these three to their chairs. I don't want them going anywhere while I decide what to do with them. Tie them very tightly."

Shawn left and returned immediately with rope. Wallace held his gun on us while Shawn tied us to our chairs.

Shawn tied my hands behind my chair. He roped my ankles to the chair legs, and wrapped several layers of rope around my waist. I could barely move.

As soon as we were tied up, Wallace and Shawn left the room.

We sat alone, awaiting our possible death sentence.

Chapter Fifteen

"Hey, Cruiser-boy," Ezra said to Hayden, "I really appreciate this mess you've gotten us into."

"Shut up, Ezra," I snapped. "This isn't the time for sarcasm. We've got to get out of here. This is real — and scary."

"What are we gonna do?" asked Hayden.

"We've got figure out a way for the morphing power to get us out of these ropes, first of all," I said.

"But if we morph into another person, we'll still be tied up," Hayden said.

"I've got it!" Ezra cried.

Without even explaining his idea, Ezra started to morph. We watched as his facial features changed, becoming larger and sharper. His hair shrunk to a crew cut.

But it was his body that went through the most amazing transformation. It grew tremendously as he sat, bound, in his chair. His muscles began to bulge and ripple.

Within seconds, Ezra had morphed into Arnold Schwarzenegger, the strongest man he could think of.

There was only one problem. He was still tied to his chair.

In fact, he was tied so tightly that the ropes were cutting into his fantastically muscled body.

"I thought I could break the ropes," Ezra wheezed, his lungs constricted by the ropes. Instead, he had made his situation worse.

Suddenly I knew what to do.

"You went the wrong way, Ezra," I said. "We don't want to get bigger, we want to get smaller!"

"How small?" Hayden asked.

"Small enough that we can slip out of the ropes. Small as a toddler."

Instantly, I wished to become as small as my three-year-old nephew, Matt. I felt the tingling as I started to shrink.

Within seconds, my clothes were huge on my small frame, and the ropes hung loosely.

"I'm thinking of a toddler, but I'm not shrinking!" Ezra wailed.

"Me, too," Hayden said.

"You're probably just thinking of a toddler in

general," I said. "The morph apparently works only when you think of a specific person. Remember when you guys were over at my house and met my nephew Matt? Think of Matt!"

In a matter of seconds Ezra and Hayden began to shrink, too. It took Ezra a little longer because he had to shrink down from Schwarzenegger size, while Hayden only had to shrink from fourteen-year-old boy size.

But soon all three of us were exact duplicates of my nephew Matt.

"Thank goodness our minds stay the same even though our bodies change," I said. "If our minds became three years old also, we'd probably just stay here and play with the ropes."

"Let's get out of here," said Hayden.

"First let's morph back into ourselves," I said. We couldn't move as fast as toddlers.

Fortunately for us, Shawn and Wallace had seen no need to lock the door, since they had tied us so securely. We slipped quickly out into the hall and tried to re-trace our steps to the exit.

Next stop, the police station.

Then I heard something. I motioned to my friends to stop.

It was Mr. Frank's voice.

" . . . the delivery," he was saying. "Yes, it's still on for tomorrow."

I put my finger to my lips to shush my friends.

I looked up, and I saw an air vent in the ceiling. Mr. Frank was in an office somewhere in the factory talking to someone, but his voice was traveling through the ventilation system.

As badly as I wanted to get out of there, I also wanted more hard information to take to the cops and our parents so they'd believe us.

"The flight to Mato Grosso takes twelve hours," Frank's voice said. "As soon as the first batch of chemicals arrive, they'll be ready to spread. Have you hired the spraying plane to spread the RF compound?"

Pause.

"My best guess is the vegetation starts dying within forty-eight hours. Within a week, nothing is left alive. Then the construction can start."

Another pause.

"I'll expect to see my payment by the end of the day, or the RF compound doesn't get shipped down there. And you can't go forward with your plans without the compound."

Another brief silence.

"How many acres?" Frank asked. His was the only voice we could hear, so he must have been on the phone.

"How many do you want to kill? One barrel should cover at least a thousand acres."

My head was spinning as I tried to put it all together.

Frank was shipping something called RF compound — that must be the toxic stuff in the barrels outside — to Mato Grosso in Brazil. There, as best as I could understand, a plane would spread it on the tropical rain forest.

One barrel would kill a thousand acres of rain forest — and there were more than a hundred barrels stacked outside. For all I knew, the factory was making even more.

Whoever Frank was talking to — probably someone in Brazil — wanted to build something. But that could only happen once the rain forest was dead

We hadn't just gotten ourselves into a jam. We had stumbled onto a plot that could disturb the natural balance of the planet!

Chapter Sixteen

"Let's get out of here," Hayden said.

I'd heard enough, and I agreed.

We ran down the hall and hit the door we thought was the exit. We had no plan about how to get past the guard at the gate.

But the door we pushed open wasn't an exit. We found ourselves in another room. Along one wall there were lockers, sort of like our lockers at Messetup, only larger. In the middle of the floor there were benches. It reminded me of the changing room for gym class.

"Swell," said Ezra. "Wrong room." He started back towards the hall.

"Wait a minute," I said. "Maybe there's something in those lockers that could help us."

I ran to the lockers and started flinging open doors. Some lockers were empty, but many contained clothes on hooks and hangers. Maybe the workers at the factory changed clothes here and put on special suits so they could work with the chemicals without becoming contaminated.

"I have an idea, guys," I said. "Look for men's suits."

We picked through the lockers quickly and found two men's suits. But there were only two. Then Ezra opened a locker and pulled out a janitor's uniform, a set of gray coveralls.

We laid them out on the floor to get an idea of their size.

"Now think of a man you know about this size that you can morph into," I told them.

"But who has to wear the janitor's outfit?" asked Ezra.

"You do," Hayden and I said simultaneously. "You found it, you wear it."

Ezra grumbled, but he didn't protest anymore.

Fortunately, my dad was about the size of one of the suits, and I started morphing into my own father.

First I had dreamed that I'd morphed into my own mother, and now here I was morphing into my own father.

Hayden morphed into his Uncle Leroy, an

overweight guy I'd seen over at Hayden's house a couple of times, usually sitting on the sofa drinking a beer.

Hayden and I looked at Ezra in astonishment. He wasn't Ezra anymore.

He was Principal Klonk. Again!

"Ezra!" I hissed. "This is no time for your goofing around! We're in serious trouble."

"I'm not goofing around this time. Klonk is the right size for this janitor's outfit."

Sure enough, he was right. As much as it bothered me, Ezra got to be Principal Klonk again. And Klonk dressed as a janitor, no less.

Even when Ezra wasn't trying to turn things topsy-turvy, he somehow managed to.

"OK, Ezra," I said. "But no joking around."

Soon Hayden and I were suited up, with our neckties tied, sort of. (Being a girl, I had never learned to tie a necktie, and mine looked pretty pathetic when I checked in the mirror. But hey, I was escaping, not trying out to be a male model in a magazine ad.)

What a strange trio we made: my dad, Hayden's Uncle Leroy and Principal Klonk dressed as a janitor.

At least we didn't look like the three teenagers

that everyone inside the factory would soon be looking for.

I took a deep breath. "Let's go," I said.

We went back into the hall and looked around, trying to figure out the way to the exit.

After some pointing and whispering, we set off to our left. We found a door and pushed it open and were greeted by sunlight. Blessed sunlight.

We were outside!

"There's the gate," Hayden said. "Let's just walk right up there like we're important guests on our way out, and maybe the guard won't ask too many questions."

We walked across the factory grounds towards the gate. As we approached, we saw the guard raise a walkie-talkie to his mouth.

"This is guard post One reporting in. I have three unidentified male adults approaching. They are not wearing authorization badges. Request instructions. Over."

Rats!

"OK, guys," I whispered to my friends as we kept walking. "There's only one way to play this. Walk right up to the guard, look innocent, and when we get close to the gate, run like you've never run before."

The guard's walkie-talkie sputtered and crackled with static as he listened to it.

The gate was a few feet ahead of us, still open.

"Now!" I yelled, and the three of us took off running.

We were suddenly aware that we hadn't chosen the best bodies for running. My dad is, he says, "only" forty-one and he jogs, so I was in pretty good shape.

But Hayden's Uncle Leroy was in his fifties and the only exercise I'd ever seen him get was by pushing the buttons on the TV remote control. And Principal Klonk wasn't going to be entering any marathons.

We ran, but it was hard work. We hit the open gate, wheezing and gasping like the middle-aged men whose bodies we had morphed into.

"Halt!" the guard shouted.

Just then, we heard an alarm go off inside the factory. It sounded like the kind you hear in a movie when a prisoner has escaped from jail.

That was us — prisoners who had escaped from a jail.

Now they knew we had escaped. And they would come after us soon.

Chapter Seventeen

We burst through the gate and made straight for the thick woods behind the factory.

We could hear the guard yelling and the alarm blaring. The guard wasn't chasing us, though. Maybe he hadn't gotten the order to abandon his guard post and come after us.

Into the woods we ran, our lungs bursting, our legs heavy. These middle-aged bodies were the pits, I thought.

It had to be even worse for Hayden and Ezra. Hayden's face (actually his Uncle Leroy's face) was as red as a tomato, and he had only run a few hundred yards.

"Just a little further, guys, and we'll find a hiding place," I said.

We finally found a good place to rest, behind a huge tree that had fallen. We could squat behind it and not be seen.

We gasped for air.

"Man, that was close," said Ezra. "This body is worthless. I'm gonna morph back into Schwarzenegger. Or Michael Jordan. Somebody who can run."

"Don't do it," I said. "If you do, your clothes won't fit. Plus, we don't want to call too much attention to ourselves. Michael Jordan walking down the street is going to attract massive attention — particularly Michael Jordan dressed as a janitor."

"So what do we do now?" asked Hayden.

"I've been trying to get to my parents all day," I said. "If I can explain it to them, and make them believe me, we can go to the police. Then I think we'll be safe."

Hayden interrupted me.

"Abby," he said. "Look at your hands."

I did. They were my own hands — Abby Moody's hands.

Then it hit me. I wasn't Abby now; I was my dad.

"What's going on?" I asked. "How's the rest of me?"

"The rest of you looks like your dad," said Hayden. "But your hands have changed back to Abby's."

"Oh no," I said. "The morph is wearing off!"

I concentrated hard on being my dad, and watched as my hands tingled and changed back to man's hands. That was close.

But what was happening? Were we losing the power?

"My legs feel weird," said Hayden.

He pulled his pants up from his ankles. We looked at his bare legs below the knee. They weren't Uncle Leroy's legs. They were Hayden's legs.

I told him to concentrate on returning to Uncle Leroy. This wasn't any time to be going around half-and-half, like some sort of mutant. What if our faces started to change, but only halfway?

We weren't out of the woods yet (so to speak). We might still need the morphing power more than ever. Besides, our parents would never believe us if we couldn't demonstrate.

But from everything I could tell, it was wearing off.

Chapter Eighteen

"Let's head to my house," I said. "We'll find a private spot and morph back into ourselves before we tell my parents. You guys can call your folks and have them come over and we'll get the whole story out once and for all. Maybe then we'll be safe."

We had to double back through the woods. We could hear sounds off in the distance like maybe people were looking for us, so we crept quietly.

The sun had gone down by now. It had been hours since I'd been called into the principal's office and met Wallace, the fake FBI agent. It was almost dark.

We made it out of the woods, and soon we were back on the main road that led from RF Industries back into town.

Night had fallen by the time we reached my street. Only one block to my house, and safety.

I had gotten over my earlier fears that if people

knew about our morphing power, they'd label us freaks, and maybe send us off to some lab to be poked and prodded by scientists.

All of those fears faded away in comparison to being kidnapped at gun point, tied to a chair and interrogated, and having someone say he was seriously weighing the possibility of killing us.

Hey, bring on those cheerleaders, I thought. Let them call me a freak. I'll morph into one of them — and that will freak *her* out.

There was my house, just ahead.

And there, parked outside my house, sat a dark blue van with smoked windows.

It was parked near a street light. We could see the tailpipe vibrating a little, a sign that the engine was running.

That meant Wallace and Shawn were in the van, and probably not in my house, asking my parents a lot of questions they would have a hard time answering.

"Do you see what I see?" asked Hayden.

"Not good. Not good at all," said Ezra.

"But they're looking for three kids," said Hayden. "We're adults, if you'll notice."

"Maybe not," I said. "The guard could have

given them the description of how we look now. Let's go to your house, Hayden."

We turned around and walked back up the street. The men in the van who were staking out my house hadn't seen us.

A quick cut-through, and there was Hayden's house.

There was *another* van, parked in front of Hayden's house.

Maybe Wallace and Shawn had split up. Or maybe Mr. Frank had a security staff with lots of men, and we'd only met two of them.

We'd told Frank our names back in the interrogation room. He'd figured out where we lived. And he was waiting for us.

Seeing the vans parked outside Hayden's house and my house was extremely creepy. It was now completely dark.

I looked at my watch: It was after 9 p.m.! My parents were going to start freaking out wondering where I was.

But if I tried to get home, I would never make it. Whoever was in that van would intercept me and take me back to the factory before I could even scream for help.

And if we went to the factory another time, I had a feeling we wouldn't be coming out again.

"My house?" asked Ezra.

"What do you think the odds are there will be a van parked outside your house, too?" said Hayden.

"The police station," I said.

We started jogging towards the police station downtown, trying not to panic. RF Industries was suddenly everywhere, and we knew they had one goal in mind — to make sure we didn't tell what we knew. At any cost.

The police station came into view as we rounded a corner.

So did the dark blue van with smoked windows parked right outside, its engine idling.

"Oh, *no!*" I moaned.

"Couldn't we somehow get past the van and into the station?" said Hayden. "Once we were inside, we'd be safe while we told the cops what was going on."

"Not a chance," I said. "He's right in front of the station. We can't get by him."

They had staked out our parents' houses and the police station. We were trapped in the bodies of out-of-shape, middle-aged people, and we'd been running and walking for more than an hour, so we were really starting to hurt.

And there was evidence that our morphing power might be starting to fade or go wacky on us.

Things looked hopeless.

Chapter Nineteen

Think, Abby, think, I told myself.

What could we do? How could we tell people about RF Industries?

We couldn't just walk into some store or ring someone's doorbell and start babbling about kidnappers with guns who were going to poison the Amazon rain forest. No one would believe such a tale.

We had to be believable. We had to get the word out. How could we do it?

Then I had an idea. It was risky. It was complicated. It would take a lot of nerve. Plus it would involve us splitting up, and I didn't like that much. There was safety in sticking together.

But it was our only hope.

I told the guys the rough outline of my plan. Some of it could be planned in advance, and some of it we would have to make up as we went along.

They agreed it was our best chance.

We turned and left the street corner near the police station and the van and started walking again.

Man, was I sick of walking.

It was funny, we were in the bodies of adults, but we couldn't drive. Even if we had a car, our brains were still fourteen years old and hadn't taken driver's ed yet. We'd probably crash before we got two blocks — particularly if Hayden and I were dumb enough to let Ezra behind the wheel.

Ezra driving a car. It was still two years away, if we made it out of this alive. But I still shuddered at the thought.

Finally, after it seemed like we had been walking forever, I saw it: WHUM-TV, Channel 12. The TV station.

The local TV news would be broadcast at 10 p.m. The entire city would be watching, since WHUM was the only TV station in our town.

If my plan worked, the entire city would learn about RF Industries tonight at 10 in a very special news broadcast.

It was now 9:45 p.m.

94

Chapter Twenty

Of course, we couldn't just walk right into the station and say, "Excuse us, we'd like to get on the news right away to talk about a conspiracy to destroy the rain forest and how some bad guys threatened to kill three innocent teenagers."

TV stations had security guards. We'd get about one sentence out and we'd be back on the street.

And for all we knew, there were more dark-blue vans with smoked windows cruising around.

So we had to use a little bit of trickery. And a lot of morphing.

I found an alley beside the TV station that was darker than any darkness I'd ever seen before. That suited me perfectly, since I needed to morph again without being seen.

I thought of the TV news anchor, John Smiley.

Soon I felt the tingle and, *boom*, I was John

Smiley. The suit I'd taken from the locker back at the factory didn't fit perfectly, but it fit well enough.

I walked back around to the front of the station and marched through the front door.

"Good evening, Mr. Smiley," said the security guard. "I thought you'd come in a couple of hours ago, sir."

Hey, I liked being a TV news anchor. People treated you with respect.

"Just stepped out for a breath of air," I lied. "Time for the news." And I strolled on into the building.

Of course, I had no idea where I was going. I knew, sort of vaguely, that there must be some sort of set with a big desk and a TV camera or two pointing at the desk. And I figured that was probably where the real John Smiley was, getting ready to read the news live.

But I couldn't go to the set yet and have John Smiley suddenly see himself walk in.

The time was 9:48 p.m.

I walked quickly down a hall, hoping I wouldn't meet anyone. They'd want to know why I was wandering around instead of getting ready to read the news.

Finally I found what I was looking for — a door to an office marked "General Manager."

Since there was at least one security guard on duty, nobody locked their doors inside the building. I held my breath, took a chance and opened the door.

The office was empty. I had guessed right. The general manager, who must be the boss of the whole TV station, went home to his family instead of staying around till 10 p.m.

The general manager's name was Greg Roberts, according to the nameplate on his desk. I walked past the desk to the window, which opened onto the back of the TV station. I opened it and whistled.

While I had been finding my way here, Ezra and Hayden had been waiting. They came running and climbed through the window.

"Where's a picture of this guy?" asked Hayden. He knew he had to look at a photo to copy Greg Roberts' looks for his morph.

"Here on the desk," I said, pointing to a picture of some guy posing with a woman (his wife, *duh*) and three small children.

Hayden picked up the photo, gazed at it, and morphed into Greg Roberts, general manager of WHUM.

I looked at my watch: 9:50 p.m. Ten minutes to go.

Ezra spoke up. "Why do I have to be the janitor?" he asked, for the tenth time since I had explained the plan.

"You're the lookout," I told him. "Now go find a mop and a bucket and get out to the lobby and be the lookout."

"But why can't one of you be the janitor?"

"We don't have time to change clothes," I explained. "I've got to be on the air in less than ten minutes, Ezra, and I'm not really sure how I'm going to do it. Now get out to the lobby and start mopping!"

Ezra was muttering to himself as he left Greg Roberts' office.

It was 9:52. Ezra had cost us two minutes. Time to get moving.

Chapter Twenty-One

I turned to Hayden.

"You've got to get Smiley off that set and keep him off for at least five minutes," I said. "Ten minutes would be better. Do whatever you have to do, but don't let him back to that anchor desk. Remember, Hayden, you're not Hayden. You're Greg Roberts, the general manager of this TV station. You're Smiley's boss. You can order him around. He has to do what you say."

"Gotcha," said Hayden. "Don't worry, Abby, I won't let you down." And Hayden left the office.

That was the last I saw of my two friends for about twenty minutes.

After we had finished our jobs, we met behind the station, and headed for home. On the way, each of us told our stories to the others. I've woven all the stories together here to give a sense of the way everything happened.

Hayden told us that he had no idea where the anchor desk was, and the TV station was full of twisting hallways. He saw a young woman walking towards him and had a brainstorm.

"Excuse me," he said to her. "I'm just on my way to the news room to talk to John Smiley. Would you please come along?"

She looked a little puzzled, but instantly answered, "Of course, Mr. Roberts."

They both stood there.

"You go ahead and lead the way," Hayden said. "I'll just be right behind you."

The woman looked even more puzzled, but set off towards the newsroom, with the fake general manager a couple of steps behind.

He saw the sign on a door up ahead: "WHUM Anchor Set. Do NOT Enter While Red Light Is Flashing."

There was red light, like a police car siren, mounted on the wall. It wasn't flashing. That would only be turned on when the news was going out live, to prevent people from going into the room and distracting the anchor while he was reading.

Hayden walked in. Smiley was sitting at the anchor desk, reading a piece of paper quietly.

"John, can I see you a moment in my office?"

"Greg? What are you still doing here? I thought you'd gone home," said the anchorman, puzzled.

"I came back cause we really need to talk," said Hayden. "Right now."

"It's five minutes till we're on," said Smiley. "Can't it wait?"

"No, it can't," said Hayden. "It will only take a minute."

"Well, you're the boss," said Smiley, and got up and followed Hayden back to Greg Roberts' office.

Meanwhile, Ezra had gone off in his janitor's uniform. He found a maintenance closet with one of those big buckets on wheels. It was full of dirty water, and there was a mop stuck down in it.

He took it from the closet and started wheeling it towards the lobby. "Why do I always get the dirty work?" he muttered to himself.

He set up his bucket in the lobby and was swirling his mop around aimlessly. The dirty water was making the tile floor dirtier, not cleaner, but the security guard ignored him.

As he looked out the glass front door, Ezra saw a dark blue van pull up in front of the station.

Two men got out, dressed in suits.

Neither was Wallace or Shawn, but they could have been their cousins. One had his hand inside his suit coat, the way Ezra had seen bad guys do on TV when they're about to pull out a gun.

They walked up to the front door and knocked. The security guard opened the door.

"The station is closed, gentlemen," the guard told them. "Please come back tomorrow."

The man in the suit drew a pistol and stuck it right up the guard's nose.

"The station is open, pal. Step back," he said.

"Come on," he said to his partner. "We got a report they may have come in here."

The clock on the wall said 9:57.

Chapter Twenty-Two

I had been lurking in the hallway, keeping my face down so no one could see it.

When I saw Hayden and the real John Smiley leave and head for Greg Roberts's office, I started towards the set.

I waited for about a minute, took a deep breath and walked in.

"Hey, that was fast, John," I heard a deep male voice call out. I couldn't see anyone though.

"What did Roberts want?" the voice asked.

I still couldn't see anyone, but felt like I should answer. "Oh, nothing. You know Roberts."

I heard laughter. At least everyone here was seeing me as John Smiley, anchorman, and not Abby Moody, fourteen-year-old girl, scared half out of her mind.

As my eyes got accustomed to the bright lights, I looked around. I moved to the anchor desk and sat down in the big comfortable chair.

I peered through the lights that were all over the place. Lights hung from the ceiling. Lights were set up on metal poles. All of them were pointing right at the spot where I was seated.

I looked up, and saw a window. It was set into the rear wall of the studio, high up, and was long and narrow. I could understand now where the voice had come from. That must be some kind of control booth where the news director or producer sat.

"Put your ears on, John," the voice said.

Put my ears on? What did that mean?

I was being given an instruction, and I didn't know what it meant. But John Smiley would have known. I was in danger of blowing my masquerade.

Then I looked down at the desk. There was a little piece of plastic that looked like a hearing aid. It was attached to a cord. I thought back to when I'd watched the news at home. Sometimes, you could see one of these earpieces in the anchor's ear.

I picked up the earpiece and stuck it in my right ear, draping the cord so it was behind me and the camera couldn't see it.

Hey, I was behaving like a real pro!

This time I didn't hear the voice in the room, just in my ear.

"One minute to air," John," the voice said.

Chapter Twenty-Three

While I was sitting down in John Smiley's anchor chair, the real John Smiley was standing in Greg Roberts' office.

He was talking to Hayden Manchester, age fourteen, but he thought he was talking to his boss.

"So what's up, Greg?" asked Smiley. "Let's make it fast."

"Uhhh, how's the family?" was all Hayden could think of to say.

"How's my family?" repeated Smiley, angrily. "You called me off the set five minutes before air to ask about my *family*?"

He took a deep breath. After all, this was his boss.

"My family's fine, Greg. And yours?"

"Oh, they're fine, fine," said Hayden.

Smiley glanced at the clock on Roberts' office wall.

"Uh, Greg," he said gently. "It's one minute till air time. I have to be on the set."

"Oh, that clock is fast," Hayden said, thinking quickly. But he had run out of things to say. He had no idea how to keep Smiley in his office.

He had to say something.

"Uh, John, I called you in here because I have some bad news," he said at last. "You're fired."

At the same time that Hayden was firing the anchorman, Ezra was watching the armed security men from RF Industries break into the station to try to stop us.

The station's security guard threw his hands into the air and started stepping backwards.

He doesn't look like he's going to play the hero tonight, Ezra thought. So it's up to me.

The two men paid no attention to the janitor as they started walking briskly across the lobby. Ezra reached down and grabbed the bucket of dirty, soapy water with one hand and pushed. It fell to its side, and gross water gushed out, gallons of it, covering the tile floor.

The men hit the water. They were wearing street shoes with slick soles. Their legs flew out from under them, and they landed on their backs.

I sat up straight in the anchor chair. A camera was wheeled up so it was right in front of me. Under the camera there was a screen with words on it. I read the words silently to myself:

"Good evening, and welcome to Channel 12 News at 10. I'm John Smiley. Now for our top story tonight . . . "

So this was how the anchorman knew what to say, I realized. Well, I was going to have to deliver a different top story than the one the station had planned.

I looked down and saw my hands.

Oh, no, I thought, not *now*!

They had changed back into Abby hands! I was John Smiley, anchor, with a teenage girl's hands on the ends of my arms.

I didn't have time to worry about morphing my hands. I had to concentrate on what I was about to say. I hoped no one would notice my hands.

"Five seconds to air," said the director, "and four. Three. Two. One."

He was silent. A red light came on the camera that was aimed at my face.

It was time for the news!

Chapter Twenty-Four

As we walked home, we continued telling our stories of what had happened to us.

Ezra said that after the two guys from RF Industries slipped and fell in the dirty water on the lobby floor, they had tried to get up.

But Ezra, playing like he didn't know what he was doing, held his mop out so it was parallel to the floor and turned around, pretending to look at something else.

As he turned, the mop handle turned with him, and caught one of the guys behind the legs as he was just getting to his feet, but before he really had his balance.

He fell again, and without thinking grabbed at the other guy, pulling him down.

The security guard watched what looked like a Keystone Kops display and finally sprang to life. He took several quick steps towards the guy that had been armed with the gun.

He had dropped the gun, and it lay in the soapy water.

The security guard picked it up and held it on the two from RF Industries. With the other hand, he reached out to the reception desk, picked up the phone and dialed 911 for the police.

The security guard looked at Ezra the janitor.

"Nice work, buddy," the guard said. "But I haven't seen you around here before. Where's Phil, the usual night janitor?"

"Uh, he's sick," Ezra said. "Excuse me." And he dashed out of the lobby back towards Greg Roberts' office.

Now it was Hayden's turn to tell.

He explained that he had told the real John Smiley he was fired because that was the only thing he could think of serious enough to make John forget about his newscast.

And it worked.

"Smiley couldn't believe it," Hayden said. "I really felt sorry for the guy. He was angry, and kept demanding to know my reasons. I couldn't think of a reason a TV station would fire an anchor, so I just hemmed and hawed around.

110

"Then he got really sad," Hayden continued. "He started begging to keep his job. I figured the best way to keep him in my office was to keep him talking, so I just let him talk, and I listened. After about ten minutes, I told him I had changed my mind, and that he wasn't fired after all. He looked at me like I was nuts, and then burst out of the office and started running for the anchor set.

"But by then it was 10:10, and it was too late," Hayden concluded.

"I didn't know how long I had," I told Ezra and Hayden. "So when the red light came on, I started just blabbing: "Good, evening, I'm, uh, John Smiley, for uh, Channel 12 news. And, uh, this is really important."

After stumbling through that, I started to relax.

"You know that abandoned factory on the outskirts of town? It's not abandoned. It's being secretly used by a company called RF Industries, and they're manufacturing toxic chemicals. They're going to send those chemicals to be dumped on the Amazon rain forest and kill thousands of acres.

"The first shipment goes out tomorrow. It's very important that the police send as many cars and officers as you can to the back of the factory, arrest everyone you can, and stop this plot.

"Oh, and one last thing. This is for the parents of Ezra Parker, Hayden Manchester and Abby Moody. I saw your kids a little while ago, and they're sorry they're late coming home, but they're safe and they'll be home soon. So don't worry."

Of course, while I was saying all this, the producer was going nuts, screaming into my earpiece. "John! John! Stick to the script! What are you *saying*?"

I had to take the earpiece out to concentrate. I don't think that made him very happy.

By the time I finished, the red light on the camera had gone off. That probably meant I was no longer on the air.

I jumped up out of the anchor chair.

"Excuse me, I think I'm sick," I shouted.

"You're more than sick, Smiley!" the producer shouted. "You're *nuts*. What the heck was that all about? We cut you off and went to a commercial right after you said that to those kids' parents."

"It's all true!" I yelled, and ran off the set.

Chapter Twenty-Five

We had done what we had set out to do. But we had no idea if it had worked.

What if the police weren't watching the news? What if everyone thought poor John Smiley had suddenly lost his mind and started raving madly on live TV about the Amazon rain forest and the old factory?

When we turned the corner onto my street, we saw one thing that re-assured us: There was a police car parked in our driveway.

Ezra's and Hayden's parents' cars were also there. But no van.

"We better morph back into ourselves before we face this," I told Ezra and Hayden. We cut into a neighbor's back yard where it was very dark, and started the morph.

Every time before, the morph had felt easy. Nothing to it.

This time it was hard.

I had to concentrate very hard on becoming Abby Moody again. I looked at Hayden, and his brow was wrinkled, like he was thinking hard, too.

But slowly he changed, and so did Ezra, and so did I, back into three eighth graders at Messetup Middle School.

"Did the morph feel different to you?" I asked them.

"Yeah, like my body didn't want to morph," said Hayden

I told them what I suspected — that our powers were wearing off. And I told them what I thought that meant — that if we successfully morphed again, we might not ever be able to get back to ourselves.

Maybe it was time to stop being Humanomorphs.

We walked up to my house. All our parents were there, and they were halfway nuts. We'd been missing ever since school let out, and they had already called the police to look for us.

Then John Smiley, the news anchor, had read our names on the TV news.

They wanted an explanation. So did the police.

So I told them. Some of it, anyway.

I told them everything except the morphing

part, because for some reason I still wanted to hold onto that as our little secret.

When I got to the part of Mr. Meanie in the van holding a gun on us, I thought my mom was gonna have a stroke.

Then I had to invent a little. I said that after we'd escaped from the factory, we figured we had to warn the town, and the best way to do that was through TV news. So we went to the station and saw John Smiley outside, and told him, and he put it on the news.

It sounded pretty believable. If the police ever questioned Smiley closely, our story wouldn't stand up.

But then *Smiley's* story would sound even more ridiculous. He'd claim his general manager pulled him off the set, fired him, then un-fired him, all in ten minutes.

What's more, his producer and the crew would all swear that Smiley had only been gone for ten seconds, not ten minutes. And there was the fact that, while Smiley claimed to be in Greg Roberts' office, thousands of people had seen him live on TV.

Only they hadn't seen Smiley. They'd seen me, in my television debut. And no one but Ezra and Hayden and I would ever know it.

The more I thought about it, though, the more I thought Smiley would probably support our story and say it was him who had alerted the whole town to the danger at the factory.

That was the only way he would get any credit for it.

Chapter Twenty-Six

The police told us that there had been a TV playing in the station, and when they heard what Smiley (that is, *me*) was saying, they sent a patrol car to the factory.

The police officer saw movement and suspicious activity, and radioed for help. Soon about six cop cars had arrived at the factory.

It appeared that everyone involved had been arrested, and the barrels of toxic chemicals had never been shipped to the rain forest.

Everyone was exhausted. Hayden and Ezra's parents took them home. My folks hugged me over and over and finally I went to bed.

This time I dreamed I was Hitler. I knew it had to be a dream, and that I hadn't really morphed into Hitler. I got up, went to the bathroom, turned on the light, looked in the mirror.

Sure enough, Hitler's face looked back at me.

My hair was black and combed down across my fore-head in a slant. I had that ugly little mustache, like a black paintbrush, under my nose.

When I looked at the rest of me in the mirror, it got freakier. I was still me from the neck down. I was Abby Moody with Hitler's head!

I ran cold water and splashed it on my face. I looked back at the mirror.

Still Hitler.

I pinched my arm several times. I didn't wake up.

My mom's voice called from her bedroom, "Abby, honey, is that you? Are you up? It's 3 a.m."

I wasn't dreaming. I was wide awake and I knew it.

I had morphed into Hitler. Was this my final morph?

Chapter Twenty-Seven

I had to change back — particularly if my Mom was going to come and investigate.

I had done a lot of explaining tonight, but explaining why I was standing in the bathroom with Hitler's head on top of my body . . . well, I didn't think there was enough explanation in the world for that.

I concentrated on turning back. I felt the tingle, only very faint. My face blurred.

Everything else faded into the background as I stared at the mirror into the eyes of the most evil man who ever lived.

Come back, Abby, I thought over and over.

The mustache quivered, then started to fade. The tingling increased. The black hair started turning brown. I was becoming Abby again.

In less than a minute, I was back to Abby. My mom never had gotten up.

That was as close as I ever wanted to come to

getting stuck as someone else. I vowed never to morph again.

The next day, on the way to school, I told Ezra and Hayden about Hitler. They said I'd been dreaming.

We walked on.

It was another day at Messetup Middle School, but not a typical day.

As we approached the steps, everyone was staring at us and pointing, talking in small groups. The brainiacs weren't in their seats; the bad boys weren't in the bathroom. They were all outside.

Waiting for us.

News travels fast. When the TV anchor reads off the names of three eighth-graders, right after he's warned the city about a threat to poison the rain forest, news travels through the eighth grade at the speed of light.

People gathered around us, asking questions. Teachers wanted to know if we were all right.

We made our way through the mob and saw Angela, Maria, Kelly and Amanda — the loathsome foursome. They tried to pretend they didn't care, that they were better than that, but eventually they broke down and joined the crowd of people who wanted to hear all about it.

The morning bell rang, and everyone headed into school. Ezra pulled Hayden and me aside.

"Listen, Hayden, this is important," he said. "This afternoon, when we all get out of class, I want you to distract Angela. Get her away from her friends."

"How come?" I asked. "Ezra, please, we've been through so much. This isn't the time for some morphing prank."

"Do it for me," Ezra said. "For all we've been through."

"OK," said Hayden. "I'll distract Angela."

As the school day dragged on, people finally got tired of talking about what had happened to us. We were cool for a while, the kids who had stopped the poisoning of the rain forest, but then things got back to normal.

The final bell rang. I met Hayden and Ezra on the front steps.

Ezra had gotten a long raincoat out of his locker, even though it wasn't raining and it wasn't that cold. It came down almost to his ankles.

Radio Ezra. Operating on his own frequency.

"There she is," he said to Hayden, pointing at

Angela.

Hayden walked over to the four cheerleaders, right past Chip. The two boys ignored each other.

"Excuse me, Angela, do you have a minute?" Hayden asked politely.

Normally Angela would have said "Hit the road, creep," and made her friends laugh. But she must have thought maybe Hayden was going to tell her some part of our adventure that no one else knew about.

Hayden put an arm around Angela's shoulder as he led her away from the group. Any other time, this would have led to a punch in the stomach, but Angela must have been dying to get some detail that no one else knew, so she could lord it over everybody else.

As soon as Angela was out of sight around the corner of the building, she re-appeared. Only now she was wearing this really ugly raincoat that came down almost to her ankles.

As she walked past, I grabbed her arm.

"Ezra, is that you?" I hissed. "You idiot!"

"It's sort of me," he whispered. "I could only morph my head. You're right, the power is fading fast. Underneath the coat, I'm still Ezra. But from the neck up, I'm Angela Kells, princess of Messetup."

Ezra walked up to Amanda, Kelly and Maria.

"What on earth are you doing wearing that skanky coat?" Maria asked.

"I was cold," said Ezra, in Angela's voice.

"Anyway, never mind the coat," she continued. "I've got something important to confess to you dudes, my very best buds."

"What? What?" the three cheerleaders asked in unison. They all leaned in.

"I can't keep this secret for another second," said Ezra. "I've had this crush on this boy for a year now. This guy is so awesome, he just takes my breath away. If he asked me to go steady with him, I'd do it in a heartbeat."

"Who? Who?" they asked, sounding like a bunch of owls. "Is it Chip? Mike? Who?"

"It's Ezra Parker," said the person everyone thought was Angela. "I have the most major crush in the world on Ezra Parker."

The three girls looked horror-stricken, as if Angela had suddenly whipped out a road kill skunk and thrown it at them.

"Ezra Parker?" said Kelly. "*Eeeewwww*!" She made a motion like sticking her finger down her throat.

"That's right," said the fake Angela. "And I want the whole school to know. I want the whole world to know! I have a crush on Ezra Parker! I love Ezra Parker! In my diary at home, I've practiced writing 'Angela Parker' over and over a thousand times!"

He was shouting at the top of his lungs.

The steps were crowded with students. They all stopped their conversations and looked at Angela Kells, the most popular girl in school, confessing her love for Ezra Parker.

"Ezra! Ezra! I loooooooove you!"

Amanda, Kelly and Maria stared at their friend, speechless.

"Well, I'm glad I finally got the nerve to tell you dudes that," the fake Angela said. "I didn't think I'd have the courage. I hope I don't suddenly get cold feet and start telling you that I didn't mean it, that I really don't like Ezra.

"One last thing," Ezra/Angela told the cheerleaders. "If I start denying I said this, I've just gone shy again about my feelings. I want you all to go make big signs and put them on my locker, saying 'Angela Loves Ezra.' Even if I tear them down and beg you to stop, promise me that you'll put fresh signs up every day for the rest of the year. Promise me that, will you dudes?"

"We promise," said the girls.

"OK, gotta run. Back in a minute."

And Ezra dashed away.

He later told me that he just barely morphed his head back into his own real head. He was behind the gym, concentrating hard on becoming Ezra again, and he missed what happened next, when the real Angela came back and re-joined her friends.

"Hey dudes, what's up?" the real Angela asked. They just stared at her.

But Ezra didn't miss walking by Angela's locker every day for the rest of the school year.

And every time he walked past, he laughed.

LOOK FOR OTHER

HUMANO MORPHS

BLASTING INTO THE PAST

Something terrible is happening to Benjamin's family. At fir it's almost too subtle to notice. His mother just doesn't look attractive as usual and his father looks mean.

The situation gets worse. Family members get sicker ar sicker. Terrified, they consult every doctor they can, but no or has any idea what is causing the mysterious illness.

The only way to save Benjamin's family is to go back in tim and undo an evil deed done by a member of Benjamin's fam many, many generations ago.

Benjamin and his friend morph into famous figures fro the past. The boys go deeper and deeper into centuries lor gone—becoming such renowned men as Abraham Lincoln ar Ulysses Grant, Julius Caesar and Marc Antony—as they ra against the clock to save Benjamin's family.